A man went to knock at the king's door
and said, Give me a boat.

—José Saramago

CONT

ENTS

vii

ON WOODEN INTERROGATIONS

Who knocks on doors anymore? Only the desperate travelling salesperson and the police, that's who—because these days, there are no more princes or gentlemen or kindnesses left in the world, merely brutes and giants who kick in doors or pound them into feathery splinters. Even devils are too polite now to raise a single disturbing fist.

TWO KNOCKS

nock, knock.

Who's there?

Witch.

Witch who?

Witch one of you can fix a broomstick?

TWO KNOCKS

nock, knock.

> Who's there?

Wood Shoe 2.

> Wood Shoe 2 who?

[Sexy Voice:] Who wood you like it 2 be?

THE MYSTICAL ADVENTURES OF THE HAPPY CAT

*I*ndeed, there he goes, the happy cat. He walks along the streets, along the canals and beside flats and businesses practically suffering with primary colors. The cat is very happy. He is a happy cat. Today, leaves dangle on the subterfuge of falling, and this is the season the happy cat likes best: when his orange coat makes him invisible and he catches colorful birds and the ugliest rats and he brings them home to his pal. When he does, his pal gives him a good hard pet and they put their foreheads together—like a head-butt, like bonding.

"What tasty snack shall I bring home today?" The happy cat spits. It makes a splash in the water and fish jump out in pretty patterns like fireworks.

*

Once upon a time, there was a little ragdoll girl and she had no eyes. Where her eyes used to be are two pale circles. Buttons used to protect her from dirt and wind and sand, but alas, one day one of the buttons fell off and another day the next one did. This is a story about a little ragdoll girl without eyes.

*

Everybody knows that the happy cat has a home, and everyone knows to whom he pledges his allegiance, and yet—when the happy cat paws at their cherry doors, someone always opens with a handful of treats. The happy cat does some paltry parlor trick, and so the nice people of Copenhagen open up cans of tuna and sardines and other aluminum sealed fish for the happy cat to eat. He is a cat with a certain *joie de vivre*, one he will share with those who are so generous to him, and everyone closes the door with smiles. After all, who could say no to such a happy cat?

In this small way, every single Danish citizen in Copenhagen is owned by the happy cat, but the happy cat remains loyal only to his pal.

*

With eyes or no, the little ragdoll girl loves to dance. Oh, she wiggles her bottom and she wiggles her top and she thrusts her ragdoll head in beat to the 808. She loves electronic music—because she just loves to dance all night long.

*

Every day now, the happy cat has a mission: to find a new pal for his pal. It isn't that the happy cat isn't enough, but recently, his pal lacks humor and he's always so somber, dolorous, just plain sad. The happy cat does not like this, so he brings home new friends for his pal, but not just any old thing deserves the privilege of being pals to his pal: oh no way, the happy cat must interview these candidates first. Most often, they are not sturdy enough, but the happy cat delivers every day, even when these new pals are already dead.

*

The ragdoll girl was once a beautiful young lady. She met a nice woman—that's me—who promised her friendship and endless devotion, and my potions are strong. When I hobble off, she waits, small and helpless, her rags like daffodils in the wind.

She is so beautiful and young and in love, and I wish she could stay so forever.

*

There is a crumpled ball caught in a spider-webbed corner of the study belonging to the man who is the happy cat's pal. If the paper were straightened out, it would say this: "Once [upon a time] (scratched out), there [was a] (scratched out) is a horses and the horse". This is all the paper says. It says nothing more. Now it is a mere crumpled ball and the spider in whose web it currently resides is very poisonous. Watch out: here it comes.

*

Quite frankly, the happy cat wouldn't touch an opossum with a fishing pole, but maybe an opossum is exactly what his pal needs—but then! Down the canal floats a little ragdoll girl, and she is soaked to the seams, and the happy cat knows it instantly: this is the *perfect* pal for his pal. He lets go of the opossum, who is quite scared. It runs off and quickly.

The happy cat also takes off running, downstream, as fast as the water is flowing and then a little faster because he must outrun the downstream momentum that holds the ragdoll girl hostage, and now the happy cat slows down some to jump down the stairs and he slows until stop! and he steadies his hind legs and wraps his claws around the cement edge and he lowers his torso downwards, towards

the river—and boy could this be a colossal mistake!—
towards the river some more, towards the ragdoll girl—and
at just the right moment, he snatches her clean up. He is
such a good cat!

✳

When the ragdoll girl dances, she drops so much molly
that diamonds sprinkle the edges of her eyes.

But even this cannot last forever, and at the stroke of
midnight, the ragdoll girl must retreat into her ragdoll girl
body, and no one would like a ragdoll girl at a party like
this, it's just such a fancy one, no, the ragdoll girl would
simply not belong.

✳

But that was long ago. Long, long ago.

Back then, the ragdoll girl had eyes, and what did they
see?

✳

Once, the ragdoll girl saw Prince Charming, but he didn't
see her—just a ragdoll girl laying along just another marble
staircase, he was sick of marble staircases. He rushes off to
do something very important.

✳

He drags the ragdoll girl by the neck with his teeth, and she
leaves a train of dirty water everywhere they go. The happy
cat is not happy with this situation that sprinkles water all
over his coat. This makes him a distinctly unhappy cat. An
unhappy cat is a terribly bad kitty.

He slackens his hold on the ragdoll girl, and her head

flops free against each and every hard cobblestone, all the way home.

*

The happy cat's pal lacks spirit, and with lack of spirit comes lack of inspiration: nothing inspires him, nothing moves him; he feels—but without emotion.

*

When I asked her what she wanted to trade, she said, "My eyes," and I just shrugged. I don't complain, and it's out of my paygrade to explain what a bad wager she's about to make.

*

But goodness did she love to dance.

*

The happy cat drops the ragdoll girl right at his pal's feet. Surely, this will earn him a wealth of treats, maybe of a few different varieties; the happy cat looks first at the ragdoll girl he has brought just for him and then he looks at his pal with his violet eyes that plead for love and acceptance. He yowls just once, to acknowledge something goddamn it, but no one responds.

Suddenly, his pal shoots his hand out and gives the happy cat's head a good hard petting. "What's this, fellow?"

The happy cat snakes around his pal's legs to express joy.

*

The happy cat's pal goes downtown and he moves with intention without being rushed. The pal stops at the baker's, just to say hello. "Hello," the pal says.

"Good morning to you, good chap," said the baker. Tell me, are you working? Are you making any kronas these days?"

The pal's head falls. He doesn't bother answering. "You're looking splendid as always."

The baker hands the pal a loaf of crusty bread and a tub of cloudberry jam.

"Oh, thank you, but—"

"I insist, I insist," and then he grabs another bag from behind the counter, "and this is for your happy cat."

"Thank you," the pal says, because he is honestly hungry.

The pal snacks on the bread and jam, and the city is busy with fall fragrance and produce. Happy Danish people bicycle along the canals and other happy Danish people sit at cafés along the canals; everyone is having a splendid day. The trees are every perfect autumn color, crispy with song.

The pal stops at many stalls and shops and every owner asks about the happy cat and kronas and soon enough the pal has an armful of goods. "Take it," they insist, all of them, and so what can he do? He cannot be rude! By the time the pal reaches the button shop, he is pushing a shopping cart and even that is overflowing. Like Odysseus finally reaching Ithaka, here is the pal, at the button shop, the whole reason for this expedition: just two little buttons.

*

Once there is a beautiful girl and she has a beautiful voice and she's something of a princess, except that she isn't royalty. As such, Prince Charming can't be bothered to look at her. She comes to me and I say, "You are despairing, I can tell." Now this is the first time we met, but for many years I have watched this beautiful girl.

"Your hair is so neatly combed and such a sonic silver,"

she says, "surely, you must be here to help me. Please, old crone lady, help me."

I promised her that the prince would see her, finally, but I did not mention the marble staircase and her new ragdoll girl body. I did not mention how invisible she would always remain.

*

There are many buttons at the button store. The pal has never seen so many buttons captured in just one place. He says to the girl behind the counter, "I must sew two eyes, but how do I choose?"

The girl takes him by the hand, and it feels like a storm in her simple touch, and she guides him to the thousands of buttons in the store. "Feel it," she says, closing the pal's fingers around a fancy gilded button, "and the right one will just be right."

The pal takes a single bright purple thread and carefully sews two eyes into place. She is perfect now, flawless.

*

The ragdoll girl jumps up and takes his hand in hers and now they are in a small barn. They stand beside this very fallow candle and it woes. It woes, "Oh, that I should only have one single purpose in my life!" The fallow candle, it would seem, has no purpose, being fallow and all that.

The melting pot calls out, "Shut up, you little brat."

"Mama," the fallow candle says, "I'm sorry."

The pal looks at the ragdoll girl because he doesn't understand how a fallow candle can be related to a melting pot.

"Just watch," the ragdoll girl says.

Now a large sheep slams his way into the barn. He splinters the wooden door.

The fallow candle jumps twice, but no flames rise to his wick. "Papa!"

The sheep looks at his fallow candle son and asks, "Why are you still here? We have no use for you."

The barn is fairly sparse. Some hay and wooden stalls, but there's enough feed in the melting pot to keep the sheep happy.

"We should just melt you, be done with you," the sheep says, and the melting pot does not disagree.

The fallow candle feels distressed. He is in crisis. He packs his bag and begins a journey and the journey will never be complete until he finds a purpose in life.

Along the way, he meets a tinderbox. "Tinderbox," the fallow candle says, "what are you doing in this forest? This place is not safe for a pretty tinderbox like you."

The tinderbox says, "What are," and she stares the fallow candle right in the eye, "*you* doing here?"

"I have no purpose in life. I am without destiny. I am useless."

"Crawl inside me," the tinderbox says and opens her lid. The fallow candle bends and distorts, but how can he jump in? The tinderbox unlatches something and a door opens and the fallow runs inside.

And so the tinderbox glows with purpose, like this is what she was always meant to do, like she was waiting for a fallow candle to grant her life.

"Do you understand?" the ragdoll girl says, and her button eyes fall off. They roll around the ground until they fall flat.

*

Don't go calling me a bully. I grant only what is asked of me. People should not speak in metaphors when what they desire is literal.

❋

They fall flat and sink into the ground. The pal palms the earth and it is completely flat.

❋

Meanwhile, the happy cat goes along his day, free of the burden of the hunt. He bakes his fur in the sun until it sets. Then, he returns to his pal because it is getting cold and damp outside.

❋

Six, but now he has only four buttons left.

❋

The pal picks two different buttons: a silver star and an olive square. The first time he had put on two matching buttons. Now he attempts a different strategy. He secures the buttons, first with thread and then with superglue. The ragdoll girl pops into life and puts her little cloth hand in his human hand, and suddenly, they are in a field and pastel flowers grow wild and untended. There is a very handsome butterfly who catches everyone's eye, and he flutters onto a dandelion. The truth is that he, too, is a desperate one. He must find a mate but none of these paltry flowers will do. He turns his nose up and flies off to another flower. And then another. And then another. The seasons change and he dies, alone. His fall is not graceful. It's just a fall. And he is just another flattened bug waiting for the soil to incorporate his body.

"Do you understand?" Her eyes fall to the ground, and he is too slow to retrieve them from the past retreating into the present.

✳

He puts his hand around the ragdoll girl's cotton hand and looks at her eyeless face. "But I don't understand yet," he says, and in walks the happy cat and his pal forgets the whole ordeal.

✳

For many days his pal has been quite happy. His mood became a spirited jig, as opposed to a requiem, which was how it was for far too long.

Nobody likes a downer, not even a happy cat.

For many days his pal was not a downer at all. His pal was as happy as the happy cat himself. Flowers thrust into bloom when he walked by their boxes, and all of Copenhagen, it seemed, rushed past Winter and flew into the apex of Spring. Colors just ached from inhabiting such beauty, such substance.

And then the happy cat found the ragdoll girl in his box of toys.

✳

Did she ever even have eyes?

Surely, this is all the pal's imagination. What else could it be?

✳

It is the only ethical thing to do: the happy cat does not let go until the water nips at his teeth. She floats off without any eyes on her face, blind.

Today the happy cat is not too happy. He catches a purple winged dove right at its neck, and its fight only prolongs the suffering. The happy cat plays.

The thing is limp and probably dead when the happy cat reaches home. His pal is waiting for him at the door. "What's this?" His pal's fingers are all black. His pal has been working, and when he is working, he is a happy pal.

The happy cat drops the dead bird at his pal's shoes. They are worn down. They used to be a glossy mustard. Now they are brown.

His pal picks him up, which the happy cat does not like one bit, and says, "Look at those dirty paws!" They go inside and the unhappy cat is still being held, and his pal takes a cold cloth to his paws and scrubs.

Very, very unhappy now, the cat goes to bed. There, nuzzled under the blanket, is a wet ragdoll girl, and she doesn't have any eyes.

*

The ragdoll girl has a curse on her—and a promise. Don't go pointing fingers: this is not my fault.

The happy cat snuggles with her and falls asleep.

There is a knock at the door. The happy cat's ears shoot up.

Ah, but it is only Prince Charming, but the ragdoll girl can't see him.

His pal bows before royalty, and the prince takes off his riding cape and unbuckles his sword because there are no beasts in here to kill.

Their affair is brief but solar.

*

The ragdoll girl dances and twirls and twists her body all around. It's a real party in there, and joy falls on the entire house, modest though it may be.

*

Now the happy cat and the ragdoll girl stroll along the canals.

Now the happy cat spots a fish-girl, and she flaps her tail and dries her hair in the sun. The happy cat and the ragdoll girl drag her back to the house. The whole way she complains and tells the most obvious stories, and everyone wishes she would just shut up already.

TWO KNOCKS

nock, knock.

Who's there?

Doris.

Doris who?

Door is locked. Why do you think I'm knocking?

LITTLE RED HOOD

If the narwhal is the unicorn of the sea, there are no unicorns on land. Many times—the rhinoceros has been confused with a unicorn, but the form and substance of their horns is quite different. Centuries ago—decades ago—merchants sold unicorn horns to apothecaries and magicians and healers to make potions and other sundry things, like love, like life itself. There are no unicorns though, weren't you paying attention? These merchants sold narwhal horns, or "the power of" captured inside those unicorns killed them until they vanished altogether. But can you keep a secret?

✳

Once—upon a time, perhaps—in the foreign land, there is an old farmer man and his wife and their little grand-daughter. She is not beautiful. In fact, she is quite ugly. The old farmer man and his wife often look at this girl with scornful beatings. She is very sad. Because the old farmer man and his wife do not care aptly for the girl, all day long she scurries around the city: riding the streetcar all the way to the Baltic Sea, which she wants desperately to call an ocean, desperately. The girl wants the water's vastness to continue and continue and one day she will swim until there is no more earth to stand on. What would happen then? Why, she will drown until her death. She will not struggle. She will accept the fate of the hideous.

This is not an act of vengeance, although indeed it would likely cause her grandparents some small degree of sadness—or even regret—or even shame—she dreams for release from her sour face and twisted smile and how her hair falls in raglan clumps.

No one has told her this, but the truth of it is that she's heard her grandparents talking all the time and they say she killed her parents, right when she was born, they saw how ugly she was and so did the doctor and so did the nurses and she was dropped right onto the floor into a pool of her own bursted placenta—she is a murderer; so many people died for her birth. The little girl, she knows sorrow. She knows loss. She is its cause and its effect, too.

✳

The whole point in having children is to suffer their inadequacies and disappointments. The whole point in having a grandchild to spoil and return her to her parents, who were once just children themselves, with the child floating on sugar and toys and toys and toys—and love, so much of it, a happy belly full. This is what the old farmer man and his wife were expecting.

When the hospital called, they had to take a ferry to Estonia, a place they already disliked, to inherit a demon baby: for what else could she be?

✳

To save themselves, the old farmer's wife sewed a hood for the baby. Every few months, as the baby grew herself into a girl, the old farmer's wife would need to sew a new one, a bigger one; the girl seems to grow without needing to be fed. And so they stopped feeding her. Demon babies who grow into little girls survive on some other substance, not food. Maybe the memory of her killing spree provides her with adequate sustenance? The old farmer and his wife do not bother with petty questions. They've given her a fine hay mattress right by the radiator to keep her warm during the snow months, which are many and barbaric.

*

The mask, of course, is crimson, a cotton-polyester blend. The old farmer's wife does not bother sewing the edges of the holes necessary for breathing and seeing and eating, even though they don't feed her, and its boundaries fray. After only a week, the little girl can barely breathe and she doesn't even bother sweeping the red thread from her eyes to see. She has nothing to see anyway. She has nothing.

*

Yes, yes, they call her Little Red Hood. They also call her: monster, devil, gorgon, etcetera, all of the same variety of savagery. And for this reason, no one has seen Little Red Hood's face in many years, as many years as she has been alive.

*

The only time Little Red Hood removes her hood is when she enters the sea. Thank goodness for the waves, or else she might have seen her own reflection!

*

When she returns home, she knocks on the door because

the old farmer man and his wife do not trust her with the key. Her hair is wrecked with salt and her skin is perfectly toasted. She is smiling, but no one can see it underneath that hood.

"Granny!" Little Red Hood runs up to her grandmother and makes to embrace her, but then she sees her and her grandmother's face turns to stone and then the rest of her turns to stone too.

Little Red Hood repeats, more quietly, "Granny."

Her grandmother's stone skin begins to crack, and Little Red Hood hugs her tightly. The stone melts like snow in the early summer. When her grandmother is fully freed, she pushes Little Red Hood to the ground and slaps her face hard.

"Go to the sea," the old farmer's wife says, "and don't come back until you have caught enough dinner for us all."

Underneath her hood, there are only tears. Salt on salt on salt.

"And if you ever call me 'Granny' ag—" But her grandmother does not need to finish her sentence. Nor can she, because Little Red Hood had already shut the door behind her.

*

Little Red Hood runs as fast as she can through the curling streets until she reaches the sea and even then she does not stop her running. Waves push her back and she just gets right up and runs further until she can't run any more and then she swims and she swims until she can't swim any more and then she sighs and drops her body down. She sinks without struggle.

*

The way the story goes is something like this: a great big whale swallows Little Red Hood up whole and from its belly grows a sorrow so large that horn threaded with scarlet pushes its way out from the whale's head. When this magical whale is discovered, it is named "narwhal."

And as for the unicorns, well, I'm sorry to say, they're not so real, not real at all.

TWO KNOCKS

*nock, knock.*

Who's there?

Madam.

Madam who?

Help! Ma dam eyelash is stuck in this keyhole.

ON THE FOUR OF SWORDS

I am a serial monogamist. Since I was twenty, I have been in three relationships.[1] Not all of them were disasters, and they all left me in disaster. Now I am thirty-five. I have been single for nearly a year. Time aches forward. I covet all I fear. Each minute is a steady stroll towards spinsterhood. This is my future, my body an effigy, almost as though the Moirai demand it.[2]

*

1. THE I, I, I, I, I, I, I. Through which the world is experienced, remembered, and underſtood. Not only vision, as the homophone wants to insiſt, but also sound, taſte, smell, touch.

2. THE MOIRAI. Also called the Fates, the three daughters of Kronos (Time) or Nyx (Night) alone, or Zeus (Zeus) or Necessity, with and without necessary combination. From the Greek, their name means *lots, deſtinies, aportioners—parts and portions, phases.* Thus, the moon has three phases.

Days after birth, the Moirai appear to decide a person's life: Clotho spins the thread, Lachesis measures it, and Atropos decides precisely when to cut it and how. The hot debate is whether or not the Moirai control more power than even the gods, and whether or not they have power over the gods, too.

The Erinyes are female chthonic goddesses of vengeance.[3] According to Homer, they exist to punish those who have sworn false oaths.[4]

Once upon a time, I swore a false oath in marriage. I married a man named Chris; I married a man I did not want to marry. I spoke words that I wanted to believe, but I could not make them true.

For many years, I blamed Chris.[5]

Today, everything weeps onto the umbrella of the Erinyes.[6]

---

3. THE ERINYES. Goddesses of vengeance and retribution; known also as The Furies. Victims call up the Erinyes in distress and in despair, and thus the curses of the Erinyes fall down upon the perps.

Not everything can be pro bono though, folks, these girls have bills to pay! When they need some work for hire, the Moirai are reliable employers. (*See* note 2.) You might be able to hide from fate, but no one evades the Erinyes. Hades and Persephone also payroll them. In the Underworld, the Erinyes manage the torture of the enforced inhabitants of the Dungeons of the Damned.

Talk about Daddy Issues: The Erinyes sprung from the blood that sprinklered off of Uranus's stump, after his son Kronos castrated him.

4. HOMER. The creator of The Simpsons, Matt Groening, gave Homer his own father's name. Then he gave his son the same name. "Simpson?" Groening winks, "short for simpleton."

5. CHRIS. Was not Christ; not a favorable crossing. Chris was cross, all the time, and cruel.

6. THE ERINYES' UMBRELLA. Some say the Erinyes were ugly monsters, as much bird as human. Instead of hair, vipers. Others insist their beauty was so enchanting that men blindly did their bidding.

To them, I bow my head, but I know I cannot be forgiven.

*

I turn to the cards to untangle love for me.

Because they use non-traditional decks, I don't know if the FOUR OF SWORDS appears, but Selah[7] & Kristen[&7]—reading separately, reading together—explain how there are three relationships in my past that I must absolve before a (fourth) LOVE I HAVE NEVER KNOWN BEFORE can enter. They tell me I must be swift. They tell me I must clean house, literally my dirty room, metaphorically my salty heart.

"Within two weeks," they tell me.

But two weeks is full of procrastination, any reason to avoid responsibility, even for love, even for A LOVE I COULD NOT YET IMAGINE—ever, it seems.

"It's time to clean," Kristen says.

Three weeks later when I leave for Chicago, my room is still a wreck. It's not that I don't believe in their magic—in my own, too—but I am too immobilized to even properly pack. The things I forget to bring, just as the things I know I need to do but don't.

And so I write this essay.

*

"Love," Selah says, "will approach quickly."

<hr>

7. **SELAH.** Appears 74 times in the Bible, frequently at the end of a Psalm. Without definitive translation, some approximate its meaning as *Amen*. To others—*Stop and listen*—a liturgical musical notation.

&7. **KRISTEN.** *Follower of X,* or *Anointed by* †.

And Kristen says, "He will not be what you expect." And Kristen says, "A scientist."[8]

"I saw that too," Selah says, and they salute each other's shared premonitions and the happy fate I will soon receive, "and you don't know him—yet."

"And," Kristen says with cautious mischief, "you will need to *teach* him how to be your lover."

In my head, I have cast myself as the slut.

✳

Chris terrorized me. Now I force myself to identify and acknowledge my participation in the reciprocation of our mutual hurt. I, too, am guilty.

✳

And so I write this essay for absolution, not my own but for those who have broken me after I have already thread-

---

8. A SCIENTIST. In his 1834 review of Mary Somerville's *On the Connexion of the Physical Sciences*, William Whewell used—for the very first time—the word *Scientist*. He didn't make it up, per se. He lays the laurels instead on *some Ingenious Gentleman*, although he was most likely being self-referential. Tell me this: was little ol' Willy modest or sly or laughably egotistical?

Before *Scientists*, science could mean either *Knowledge* or *Study* or both. But: *One who conducted scientific research* could either be a *Natural Philosopher* or a *Man of Science*. Wee Willy Wee-well (so humble so clever and so bright), in addition to *Scientist*, also minted the terms: *Physicist, Linguistics, Consilience, Catastrophism, Uniformitarianism*, and *Astigmatism*. And though fellow-scientist and colleague Michael Faraday gets the credit for the terms: *Electrode, Ion, Dielectric, Anode*, and *Cathode*, it is *somehow* common knowledge (honest truth!), each one was at Wee Willy's suggestion.

- e d   myself back together too many times.

✻

Selah, Kristen, and I get matching tattoos:
Mary Magdalene Pray for Us.[9]

✻

In the traditional Rider-Waite Tarot deck, THE FOUR OF SWORDS depicts a knight in repose.[10] His hands rise in prayer, even though he is no longer living. Three swords hang ominously over his body. A gold sword rests horizontally beneath him. THE FOUR OF SWORDS demands rest for all that is to rush forth.

✻

Pray for us, patron saint of marred women.

✻

Before I was a marred woman, I too was innocent and frail. I fell in love with Adam,[11] who God sculpted

---

9. MARY MAGDALENE. *The apostle of Apostles.* Mary Magdalene, patron saint of whores and marred women. But before that, Jesus had to exorcise seven demons from her body. It took seven tries to rid her of that pungent stink of sin.

Her skull, a piece of forehead flesh and skin (once touched by Jesus after his resurrection), her tibia, and her left hand: the (four) relics that remain of Mary Magdalene.

10. RIDER WAITE. *Ride-or-Wait?*

11. ADAM. *The first human, a man molded of clay.* But my name is not Lil-ith (and not Lil-eve); we did not "marry" Adam.

　　NOT TO BE CONFUSED WITH ATOM. *From the Greek,* meaning *indivisible, undividable, uncuttable;* an apropos word until in his own image:[12] godlike in beauty. Adam was my first love. We were so young then, so open. Adam used to tell me I had fire in my belly.

✳

The Harpies[13] steal food from evil-doers while they are eating and deliver them to the Erinyes to dole out a fitting punishment.

When we ended, Adam delivered me to Chris and then

1897 when J. J. Thomson discovered the electron, which he'd originally called *Corpuscles*. Atoms can hitch onto one of more other atoms to form molecules or crystals, and the attachment and detachment of atoms from each other causes almost every physical change observed in nature. The scientific study of this change is called Chemistry.

AND NOT TO BE CONFUSED WITH ATOM (the smallest possible unit of time). According to 1 Corinthians 15:52, an atom is the duration of time required for *the twinkling of an eye.*

12. GOD. The quaint city of Göd, northeast of Pest, thrives on its natural thermal spa with rich mineral waters.

It's the idyllic destination for those who want to escape the bustle of Budapest. That's the sell. Sure, Budapest is renowned for its bathhouses, its pools of luxury and relief, glowing steamed skin, dancing the night away: it's a real scene. For the tourist wanting to escape the scene, Göd is accessible by bus, train, or car. Although categorized as a dormitory town—commuter town, bedroom community, exurb—Göd is hardly sleepy. It has civil organizations, churches, galleries, clubs, and even its own monthly newsletter!

13. THE HARPIES. Born of the destructive wind, half-bird, half-woman: bird of body, with the breasts and sex and haggard faces of old crones. They are notoriously and factually ugly. The Harpies are a criminal delivery service, employed by the Erinyes.

I understood vengeance.

✳

Two weeks to the day, I meet a chemist.[14] I think it is fate, but it is only a coincidence. His life is complicated—or I did not clean my room.

Finally, yesterday, I cleaned my room, but it is too late already.

✳

The Erinyes [or Furies] go in search of those who have killed their family. I did not kill my dead sister: I was too late to save her. Nor did I have that power.

✳

For ten days, I watched the Moirai spin their threads around her in saline drops and plastic tubes. Clotho[15]

---

14. Chemist. Derived from Alchemist. Let us begin with the phenomenon of burning. Since long before the Greeks and Romans, fire was recognized as a mystical force that could change one substance into another, and no one quite knew how it worked, nor its capacity, nor its capability, nor its limit. We can credit fire for the discovery of iron and glass. But the discovery of gold hammered the world into submission, into devotion, and thus was born alchemy.

Chemistry has changed forms many times before and after it was "begun in earnest in 1783, with Antoine Lavoiser's Law of Conservation of Mass," (the chemists say). What will it transform into next? Turn up the heat to find out.

15. Clotho. *Spins life.* But really, it's just some thread. She comes equipped with a spindle. Although her sisters and Hermes participated, Clotho is credited for the creation of the alphabet.

extended the thread of life for my sister.[16] Lachesis kept careful books of the thread of life my sister was allotted.[17] And then Atropos cut the thread. This was the day I met Harold.[18] I thought the Fates had sanctioned our love with my sister's death, an exchange, but it was only the beginning of the looming of inevitable doom and destruction.

I have not recovered from the Moirai's gifts.

※

In Chicago, Feliz reads my cards.[19]

I ask about love, and the cards only reveal the insecurities I embraced after reading at the University of Chicago. Lauren Berlant appears in my cards—

---

16. SISTER. A sister's vows are simple, whereas a nun's vows are solemn. For a vow to be "solemn," the Church must recognize it as such. Any vow not sanctioned as solemn is considered "simple."

17. LACHESIS. *To obtain by fate, by lot, or by the will of the gods.* She comes equipped with a golden rod, with which she measures the thread straight off the spindle, and Lachesis determines destiny.

There's also a genus of venomous pit vipers named *Lachesis,* more commonly known as *bushmasters.* The average adult is 7-9', some getting as long as 14' (yes, those apostrophes are feet, fourteen feet, take a breath: fourteen feet), earning *Lachesis* some nice superlatives: longest genus of venomous snake in the Americas and longest genus of viper in the world. Their tail ends with a horny spine, which can vibrate when activated. *Lachesis* are also nicknamed *the mute rattlesnake.*

18. HAROLD. From *herald, a messenger* bringing news; a sign that something sits at the precipice, about to—.

19. FELIZ. *Happy, lucky* (yes!), *fortunate.*

—again and again.[20] And then the FOUR OF SWORDS falls.

*

The Moirai are more popularly known as the Fates; the Erinyes are also called the Furies. The Harpies have bird bodies and resplendent female faces.[21]

*

If Charming[22] were to knock at my door, I have learned not to answer. I have learned what love can achieve—what it will destroy, too.

*

At the University of Chicago, Jackie and **I** lead a workshop called "Trauma Monsters and Magic.[23]

---

20. BERLANT. From the Arabic word for *diamond*.

Lauren Berlant—scholar, theorist, friend—known most for her book *Cruel Optimism* and her contribution to Affect Studies.

21. THE HARPIES. For the most part, *written* renditions of the Harpies glorify the magnitude of their butt-ugliness. For the most part, *artistic* representations of the Harpies emphasize their unreasonably beautiful faces. Which is the more correct: what the eye sees or what the brain imagines?

22. CHARMING. A constituency in the Yau Tsim Mong District in Hong Kong, estimated population of 342,970.

23. JACKIE. Meaning: *God is gracious* or *holder of the heel* or *supplanter*. Diminutive of Jacqueline and Jacob, hipster sibling of Jack. In fact, her mother was obsessed with Jackie O. Jackie kept her mother's penchant for obsession and her father's surname, Wang. The most common surname in Mainland China. A survey from 2018 counted over one million Wangs in China.

We ask the students to write down a traumatic moment, which we then burn. We watch paper distend into ash. Then, using psychomagic, each student draws a tarot card to recast their trauma as a method to fathom the past in order to heal the present.

Again, I pull THE FOUR OF SWORDS.

*

Anne Carson translates of Sappho:[24&24&24]
  Because I prayed
  this word:
  I WANT.

*

THE FOUR OF SWORDS demands my rest, as preparation. For what—for who—for whom?

*

---

24. ANNE. Meaning: *Favored.* The Virgin Mary's mom.

&24. ANNE CARSON. Classicist, poet, playwright, translator, essayist, scholar—holds citizenship in Canada and Iceland.

&24. SAPPHO. Facts: Sappho was an archaic Greek lyric poet from the Island of Lesbos; recognized in the canon of Nine Lyric poets of Hellenistic Alexandria; aka *The Tenth Muse & Poetess.* Today, Sappho remains in fragments—and her queerness stamps language.

In which I negate prophecy.

✻

I want to answer, desperately. I want there to be a knock at my door. I want it to be Charming. I WANT, I WANT:

I WANT.

DRAMATIS PERSONAE (I)

I
Sister
Jackie
Selah
Kristen
Feliz
Lauren Berlant

*

Chris
Scientist
Chemist
Charming
Harold

*

Homer
Rider-Waite
Anne Carson
Sappho

*

The Moirai
Clotho
Lachesis
Atropos
The Erinyes
The Harpies

*

Adam
God
Mary Magdalene

DRAMATIS PERSONAE (II)

Adam
Anne Carson
Atropos
Charming
Chemist
Chris
Clotho
Feliz
God
Harold
Homer
I
Jackie
Kristen
Lachesis
Lauren Berlant
Mary Magdalene
Rider-Waite
Sappho
Scientist
Sister
Selah
The Erinyes
The Harpies
The Moirai

DRAMATIS PERSONAE (III)

Adam
Atropos
Berlant, Lauren
Carson, Anne
Charming
Chemist
Chris
Clotho
(The) Erinyes
(The) Harpies
I
Feliz
God
Harold
Homer
Jackie
Kristen
Lachesis
Mary Magdalene
(The) Moirai
Rider-Waite
Sappho
Scientist
Sister
Selah

DRAMATIS PERSONAE (IV)

Adam
Berlant, Lauren
Carson, Anne
Chemist
Chris
I
God
Harold
Homer
Molina, Feliz
Nelson, Kristen
Rider-Waite
Sappho
Saterstrom, Selah
Scientist
Sister
Wang, Jackie

*

*

Atropos
Charming
Clotho
(The) Erinyes
(The) Harpies
Lachesis
Mary Magdalene
(The) Moirai

DRAMATIS PERSONAE (V)

Adam
Atropos
Berlant, Lauren
Carson, Anne
Charming
Chemist
Chris
Clotho
(The) Erinyes
(The) Harpies
I
God
Harold
Homer
Lachesis
Mary Magdalene
(The) Moirai
Molina, Feliz
Nelson, Kristen
Rider-Waite
Sappho
Saterstrom, Selah
Scientist
Sister
Wang, Jackie

DRAMATIS PERSONAE (VI)

Feliz
Homer
I
Jackie
Kristen
Lauren Berlant
Rider-Waite
Sappho
Selah

✻

Adam
Atropos
Charming
Chemist
Chris
Clotho
(The) Erinyes
God
Harold
(The) Harpies
Lachesis
Mary Magdalene
(The) Moirai
Scientist
Sister

TWO KNOCKS

nock, knock.

Who's there?

Dolly.

Dolly who?

Dolly, Parton my French, but open the Fu@&!n' Door!

THE LITTLE MATCHSTICK BOY

*O*nce, he had to jam his fingers onto his tongue for relief. When he did so, he dropped the candle, which dropped down and down, which started the greatest bonfire the country had ever known. The people danced, and he was celebrated. And then God made rain and the palace was saved. The little boy grew to become a knight who saved distressed damsels all day long.

A girl might've been staked and then burned; the event would've been named a level four catastrophe, akin to a terrible earthquake, and the people would've spit at her tortured face behind all those licking flames. She might have been screaming, but no one could hear a thing amidst the cheering and joy. Surely, she would've been ugly, too, and there would've been no rain to save her, not a cloud in the sky.

Where does God live when there are no clouds?

THE LITTLE MATCHSTICK GIRL

*O**nce,* there was a girl and she held in her small hands tens of thousands of matches. She lit the candles, one by one, and hoisted the gilded chandeliers up, but when the party began, her fingers were blackened and she wasn't invited anyway.

Embarrassment does not need publicity, this is what adults understand and children misrepresent: the cruelty of altruism, its shine.

TWO KNOCKS

nock, knock.

Who's there?

Honeybee.

Honeybee who?

Honeybee a dear and open the door.

ONCE, SOMEONE

*I*n a land of some distance, there lives a maiden who was once a girl and her cat. The cat is named Bear because when begging for treats, she would raise her body towards the hand above her and balance herself gingerly. Other times, the cat would eat right off the maiden's hand! But always, it is a mess. Bear is a messy consumer, taking the whole in her mouth and letting the excess fall free. Later, yes, she eats those bits too. She may be a mess, but she wastes only what she does not want.

The cat is something special. She is pink all over, not a spot of another color, except the pupils of her eyes, which are black of course, but its iris, too, is pink.

What sort of pink? Why, Fairy Tale Pink, of course! It seems absurd for there to exist a color called Fairy Tale Pink, and yet—and yet—it is a soft pink color resembling typical fairy outfits in magic stories. The source of the color is in the Pantone Textile Cotton eXtended (TCS) color list, color #13-2802 TCX—Fairy Tale. This is all real. This is as true as words can ever become.

Once, long ago, the maiden was not a maiden but a wife. The husband over months and years turned into an ogre, and twice he tried to eat her, but at last she cut up his body and sent him to the recycling plant, hoping that something better might become of him.

Shortly after, a barrister courted the maiden, but he was allergic to cats and found himself surrounded by many other maidens who had not one single cat and it was with them that he made his bed. For this, the maiden trapped herself in sadness.

But before, long before the maiden became a wife, there was another. He was kind and handsome as they always are, and together they found a love so primary, so nascent and bright, that they parted. They parted and they forgot— but they didn't. What does she call him? Adam, the first.

Now, the maiden laces her hands with a man who cannot love, but he cares for her and that perhaps is enough. *Yes*, she thinks, *there is nothing better for me in all this world.*

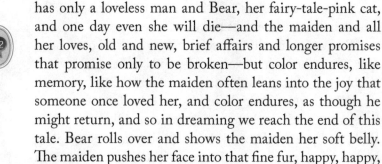

This is a story of the deficits of love. Now the maiden has only a loveless man and Bear, her fairy-tale-pink cat, and one day even she will die—and the maiden and all her loves, old and new, brief affairs and longer promises that promise only to be broken—but color endures, like memory, like how the maiden often leans into the joy that someone once loved her, and color endures, as though he might return, and so in dreaming we reach the end of this tale. Bear rolls over and shows the maiden her soft belly. The maiden pushes her face into that fine fur, happy, happy, and this is how our story ends, not with romance, never with romance, and perhaps that is fine enough.

TWO KNOCKS

nock, knock.

Who's there?

Bee.

Bee who?

[Sexy Voice:] It wood bee-hoo-ve you to let me in.

THE MATCHSTICK KILLER

According to Mrs. Watkinson, it was "dark and stormy" that night, but we all know that's bullshit because every night is dark and furthermore it was a full moon. The storm she may have been referencing—look, I'm giving her something like credit, OK?—was a blizzard earlier that day, made the whole place glitter by sunset. So it wasn't dark or stormy but it was cold, cold as a penguin without feathers, cold as a naked bear. On my notepad, I write, "Real cold." I cross it out, write, "Real fucking cold."

I've got to take this back from the start of it all, which is fine by me—case never sat right with me in the first place—but Old Sissy's been sore about it all day. Just this morning Old Sissy was all, "It's like you *want* a headache," and I was like, "It's new evidence," and Old Sissy was like, "You just want them to be connected," and he was right: I yearned for it, for him: the Matchstick Killer.

Here's the way my story goes, right? The Matchstick Killer always comes out lurking around Christmas time, and he picks a special little girl as his victim. I don't have all the details worked out just yet, but somewhere in there he freezes her to death, burns her fingertips away because he thinks this is 1995 or some shit, and puts her outside of a random family's window. His calling card: a pile of used matchsticks.

Used to be I had a couple problems with what Old Sissy calls my *theory*. First, there was only one. Can't exactly be a serial killer with just one kill. Next, lack of evidence. But let's just think through this logically, OK? Coroner says the girl died of hypothermia and when I asked her for it plain speak she went, "She became like Frosty," and so I followed, "Ho ho ho," but neither of us laughed afterwards. But today, everything's changed. Today, there's another girl.

Last night, like that night last year when the first girl appeared, was cold, real cold. Old Sissy couldn't even get his smoke lit for all the wind, and the snow was so new it felt like cotton candy.

I cross out "fucking," and Old Sissy knocks my head and says, "You writing a novel or what?" I look up all mean eyes, but Old Sissy doesn't care much about my eyes, so he goes, "Enough writing, Sherlock." Old Sissy laughs. He loves it when he gets to call me "Sherlock" because that's actually my name and the irony is so great it kills him. Most of the time he calls me "Sheryl." He swats the pencil out of my hand.

"Hey," I say, and pick up the pencil, honestly offended, and then I notice something about Old Sissy, something I've never seen before. His fingers, the tips were blackened, just like the girls'. My brain starts doing some flips, and I'm putting one against one until they pop into a bigger one, and then I go, "No way."

Old Sissy looks confused and I don't have the time to explain my head to him so I say, "Look at your fingers," and he does and he doesn't see anything so he shrugs to show me he doesn't get it and I go, "No one burned them."

Old Sissy still looks confused and I can't believe he's so dense: it's like he needs me to admit I was wrong, that there's no Matchstick Killer and it's all just a coincidence. "They were just cold," I yell. I pull the hat off my head and throw it down. I turn around so no one can see my eyes start to sheen, and Old Sissy goes, "Bat's hell, they weren't," and he throws a fresh manila folder onto my desk.

With the eraser end of my pencil, I open the folder.

THE BIG FISH LET OUT A SIGH
AND HIS LIFE WITH IT

ere there is a wife and her husband and they are very poor. They are so poor, in fact, that they cannot even buy a proper pole with which to fish, nor nylon thread for netting. The house they call their own once belonged to a merchant who pitied them greatly, so he allowed them to rest in his home during the cold winter months, and when the sun made light last longer than dark, he gave them a tent to pitch along the sandy beach of his lake. One day the merchant died, as merchants sometimes do, and because he had no family, the wife and her husband buried his body underneath the shadows of a large juniper tree. Both the wife and her husband said gentle words of gratitude and praise for the merchant and wished him comfort wherever the body goes when it no longer lives. Years pass, as they do, and soon tulips fight against frozen soil to bring color to the merchant's grave, and the woman and her husband live in his old house. Every morning they open the heavy drapes, and the sun provides light and heat and the couple care for each other dearly. They remain poor, of course, but they do not quarrel and every night they fall asleep in embrace.

One morning the husband is hungry and there is no food left to eat. He says, "Wife, I will love you forever, I promise, but forever will not be very long without food to give me strength." He reclines and places a boney hand on his forehead. The clothes he wears belonged to the merchant, and on the husband's body, they look enormous.

The wife goes out to the Danube and wades until the water surrounds her waist. She plunges her hands under the surface and sings, "Fish, o fish, I will put you on a dish. I will cover you in salt, and no one will be at fault!"

A small fish swims into her hands. She lifts it out of the water and inspects it.

The fish says, "I am only scales and bone, dear lady. Let me go and grow and next time, you can make a feast of me."

Fish are terribly honest, and so the woman returns it to the river.

Scarcely a minute goes by and another fish swims into her hands. She lifts it out of the water. This one is hardly bigger than the first. The woman says, "You are only scales and bone, dear fish. Why don't I let you go and grow and next time, I will make a feast of you?"

Fish are also quite reasonable. It winks at her, and she opens her hands to let it go free.

The woman stands in the lake for many more minutes, and her fingers grow numb from the cold. A zephyr spins the woman's brown hair towards the sky, but her eyes remain tranquil. Soon, the woman is tired and chilled and ready to retire for the day, when a big fish swivels right into her hands. It is so large she must use her arms to encircle the thing. "There, there," she says, petting the beast.

The big fish looks at her with its big fish eyes. They are not full of sorrow or defeat. It says, "You are a good woman.

Listen to me carefully and follow my instructions because I am the luckiest fish you could ever catch."

The woman nods to show compliance.

"Take me from this lake and into the old merchant's house. Cut me into eight pieces and sauté me in butter and garlic and Himalayan sea salt. Serve two pieces to your husband, two pieces you must give to the mare who is nearly starved in the stables, two pieces you must bury at the grave of the man whose house gives you shelter, and the last two you should throw to the bitch covered in fleas," the fish says. "You should also brush her hair from time to time." With that, the big fish let out a sigh and his life with it.

The woman makes her way out of the lake, and she struggles because the big fish is so big and dead and he is surreptitiously heavy. Twice she lost her footing on a slick rock, and once she nearly dropped the fish, but it fell into her floating skirt and so nothing was lost! She is full of fortune!

When her husband sees her approach with such a large specimen, he jumps from the couch, and in doing so stretches a muscle in his back. "Poo!" he exclaims and falls backwards.

*

The woman carefully skins the big fish, sprinkles pink Himalayan sea salt, grinds peppercorn onto its flesh. She melts butter in a skillet and cooks it perfectly. She divides the fillets into eight equal pieces. It is so very fragrant, and her belly grumbles. The woman stands in the kitchen, and she is faced with two choices: she can listen to the fish or she can eat. It is not just her husband and the horse and the old fleabag bitch who are hungry. She herself is starved.

What harm could truly come, she wonders, if she ate just a small portion? The fish, she figures, told her to give others two portions of his body, but he never said they had to be full portions. "I'm listening to a fish! Ridiculous!" The woman tosses her hands up in disbelief. Nonetheless, she follows the big fish's instructions. She does not take a portion for herself.

First she brings her husband his dinner. In addition to the fish, she had fixed him a baked potato and some broccoli casserole. Her husband smacks his lips and slyly eyes her plate. He must notice that there is only fish on his plate, and he drives his fork into the flaky flesh and shovels it into his mouth greedily. The woman, on the other hand, slowly eats her vegetables, savoring the flavor and pretending it might be something else. Her husband asks for seconds, and the woman is once again faced with two choices. "Ain't no more fish, honey bear, but there's plenty more else."

"Fish big as that and there ain't no more?" Her husband raises his eyebrows like he's being conned.

The woman, being cunning, says, "That fish was nothing but bones and old poo. You got all the meat there was." She points to her plate. "See here I didn't get not even one piece."

Her husband makes grunt and says, "I'll take some cake then."

The woman has not made a cake.

The woman will go bake a cake—later, after the rest of the big fish has been properly distributed.

First the woman clears the dining room table. Then, she calls the dog. She throws two pieces of fish out the back door, and the bitch races after it, her tail swooping and looping. Next, the woman wraps two pieces in a napkin and puts the last two in a bucket. She puts the napkin in the pocket of her smock and takes the bucket to the old horse. She throws a few rotten apples and carrots in too. After the horse finishes, the woman goes to the merchant's grave beneath the juniper tree and she uses her hands to dig a shallow hole. Afterwards, she returns to the kitchen, cleans the dirt from under her fingernails, and begins baking a cake.

✳

Even though Bratislava is the capital of Slovakia, it's hardly even a city. It's the kind of place the woman and her husband can live without too much bother, but they'd probably take constant pestering if it meant eating more often. The woman is now very hungry; now she is the one who is all bones and skin, but at least her skin is not scaly! No, her skin is smooth from goat's milk baths.

✳

A month passes and then another. Every day, the woman regrets her decision to not eat that stupid fish. It was the last meal with fresh meat she cooked, and she didn't get one bite.

TWO KNOCKS

ốc cốc.

Ai đó?

Cam.

Cam nào?

Cam ơn bạn đã mở cửa.

TWO KNOCKS

 *nock, knock.*

Who's there?

Spell.

Spell who?

"W"—"H"—"O"

THE DEVIL'S HEAVY BRIEFCASE

ere there is a man, his second wife, and the man's young daughter. The man is a hearty German man and his second wife is a looker, sure, but beauty leeches onto his daughter and enlivens even her simple gestures with dance.

When the man brought his second wife home and she for the first time witnessed his daughter's grace, shadows radiated in the second wife's heart. Her heart, once bright and thumping, became the opposite of a sieve: it grinds in spicy peppercorns and pumps out this new substance, this non-blood blood, this barely viscous sludge, all around her body and back into her heart. Her very composition changes: instead of water, brutal tar. And so her skin radiates.

As though mere proximity to the man's daughter makes a swan out of the second wife.

Together, they live in a modest home in the suburbs, and they live in peace.

The man goes to work every day.

Meanwhile, at home, the second wife cleans house and cooks meals and tends the garden and washes the clothes and hangs the clothes outside and brings the clothes inside because of rain and hangs the clothes inside and this happens every day—why can't she see the pattern?—and the clothes don't dry inside too well but she is only a second wife, what else can she do? Every day the second wife also rinses the dishes and loads the dishwasher and unloads the dishwasher and braids her husband's daughter's hair and bakes cookies and teaches her husband's daughter her lessons and mends and sews and shines the windows and sweeps the floor and swiffers the floor and dusts and folds and makes all the beds in the house, modest though it may be.

And over time, the second wife comes to think of her husband's daughter as her own. She turns to love her, even. And so every morning the second wife wakes early to enter the forests to fetch fresh dahlias to weave into the girl's hair. The city itself is a city, yes, but the man and his second wife and his daughter live at the very edge of town, where the forests cleave toward the sky and its canopy makes the earth an invisible black. The second wife can only spot dahlias from the shimmer of dew.

This is a frightful forest, one occupied with monsters and wandering spirits, but the second wife finds enough dahlias every morning, and swiftly, she retreats to the safety of her stepdaughter's embrace. The flowers are not poisonous; they bloom bright colors that portend spring when caught against the glint of sunlight. The second wife thinks her good daughter has cured all the darkness out of her, such is the infection of her glowing purity. And so she cherishes the little girl.

❋

When the husband brings home meat, which is rare because they are quite wretchedly poor, the second wife gives the best cut not to her husband but to the girl. Perhaps the husband is jealous of this, perhaps not, but watch carefully as this scene moves forward and judge for yourself the terrors that curdle when no one is looking.

✤

One night there is a knock at the door. Who could it be?

The devil walks in. He is not red. He does not have horns or a tail. He wears a charcoal tailored suit, glitter shoes, and carries a leather briefcase. When the devil puts his briefcase on the table, its legs collapse from the weight. This is the first indication that the man who has just entered is the devil.

Although to be fair, the table is old and its legs already had a sway. Everything in the house is old and used up. The house itself is full of mouse holes and it's hard to say if there are more ants or dust on the ground. The devil pats down his pants and ants go flying. The devil's face shows his distaste for being put in such a circumstance as theirs.

The only man who can carry such a briefcase with ease must be the devil. This is the man's logic.

He offers the devil some dinner. He says, "Unfortunately, I have forgotten to pick up a fresh cut of meat. We have only vegetables for you, but my second wife has cooked them splendidly." The man glares at his wife.

The second wife says, "It is only a humble meal, and this is by no fault of my husband. I apologize for my own inadequacies."

The devil smiles warmly. He says, "Gladly."

✤

Earlier in the day, the man had left for work. He works all the way downtown. The man is not a worker but a beggar.

He does not tell his second wife and his daughter that he is a beggar—it's a matter of pride, you see—because he is a man who is fully absent of talents and so when he leaves in the morning, he goes straight for the place of spirits and walks off with a small portion of vodka, which he drinks immediately and demands another. "If only you had another mark or two, but I have nothing here for you, you fool," the man of spirits says.

Every morning, the husband says with optimism, "I have no coins, but I have a second wife who is not half bad." He is bargaining and a jerk. Every day he has offered this bargain and every day he is declined.

The man of spirits says, "Yours is a kept woman, and she will not change keepers so easily."

"And for my little daughter?" the man asks. Perhaps this is an act of desperation—or, there is something sinister in this father that no one else can see save this man of spirits. Now the man of spirits has few ethics, but even he will not take an exchange of such youth for just a mouthful of spirits.

Some days, the man of spirits feels pity for a man who would trade his only daughter for a few swigs of vodka. Those days, he donates a little extra to the man. Other days, the man of spirits feels revolted by the whole exchange. Those days, the man gets nothing. He leaves the spirits shop with his head hung low, not for shame, per se, but for shame that his skills of persuasion are so lacking.

*

The man tells his second wife and daughter that he is an engineer and works at BMW.

Instead, after he leaves the spirits shop, he goes to a bustling corner and sits against an old brick building and props up a sign that says, "POW BEATEN AND STARVING HELP." The man has never been to war, but he looks like shit and some days he makes enough for a nice slab of meat. Pork, not beef.

Today, he has not made enough for even a chicken breast.

*

All of this occurs on the streets of downtown, where rain intermittently gives texture to the droll brick buildings and everything is brown, an ugly used-up brown. There are times that the man worries that his second wife or daughter may catch him, but it is too far to walk and they do not own a bicycle and he has taken the only car.

The devil watches. He must be ever ready to parcel appropriate punishments. A man's time always expires, so must a woman's; the devil smacks his canine tongue.

*

Tonight, the devil sits on a chair and the table is fully broken from the weight of the briefcase and he eats his meal without emotion. They eat with their bowls of creamed corn and wheat and whatnot on their laps. They use burlap napkins and their edges are frayed. The man takes notice and immediately chides his second wife and daughter. "You're making me a fool of me in front of this great man," he says, and the devil says, "Be at ease. No one is here is as fool as *you* is."

The man is confused and offended, *but he is the devil*, he thinks, *and* no one *is going to go and disrespect the devil*. This man will not be the first. After dinner, no one is full and no one is content: the food was prepared for three, not four, and the second wife eats least of all.

All of this the devil watches with care. He says, "Your daughter is quite fetching. I will take her as my chambermaid. I will train her in acts of submission, and then I will use her."

The man erects swiftly and says, "Surely you don't think I will just give you my one and only daughter!" He puts his eyes on the briefcase in such an obvious way that even an imbecile wouldn't be fooled—at all. If this were a game of Texas Hold 'Em, well, let's just say he'd be as broke as he actually is, that's not funny, sorry. His is a face of betrayal and rapacity.

The second wife sees his eyes fall to the precipice of greed. She waves her arms and runs to her husband. She pleads, "Don't do this."

But it is the daughter who steps forward, little girl though she still is, and places her hand on the devil's own hand, and she says, "My father is only a beggar and a fool. You have my consent. You are my owner." She reaches up to kiss the devil, but he is too tall and does not bend down.

Suddenly, the man is either aghast at the proposition or at his daughter's accepted harlotry. "She is too young," he says. "No, absolutely not, no way. You do not have my permission and she's a minor. And not just a minor, she's a child!"

"Well then," the devil says, "I'll just take this here briefcase and be off." He removes his hat as if to bow.

"Wait."

The whole room torpefies in anticipation: even the ants stop their scrambling.

*

Now, the man can act in a number of ways.

In one version, the devil and his briefcase leave.

Although no one but the devil himself knows what's inside that briefcase, the man knows—he just knows—that it must be something of grand value, and so he will spend the rest of his days resentful of his daughter for the life contained within the possibility of the briefcase. He and his second wife could have been happy. They could have been rich. They could buy themselves a place downtown, a flat overlooking a busy square and above a bakery, one with shingles and a staircase. They could hire a maid to clean during the day and at night the husband could demand both his second wife and his maid provide him with pleasure. Some nights, in this future that could've only been possible if only the devil and his briefcase hadn't left, he would only watch the two of them go at it. Other nights, they must fight each other to prove the greatness of their desire for him and him alone. They must be fierce and he will always secretly hope the young hot maid wins. Sometimes he will handicap his second wife. Eventually he will handicap her by cutting off her head, and then he will find a younger woman to marry and fight against the maid. Surely, you didn't think he'd marry a maid, don't be daft. Through all of this, the man will harass his daughter for all that he has sacrificed for her. For her. One day, long in the future, when the daughter is all grown, he will put a maid's outfit on her and force her to battle against his second wife. That crazy old bitch just won't die no matter how many times he cuts off her head because she is a witch with the power to grow her head back infinitely and at will. But the second wife cannot harm the girl who is now a woman and perfectly so, and the man beds the victor and his enormous German cock will rip his daughter's hymen clean off. His second wife will be crying, but it will not be for jealousy. Out of sadness, the second wife will cut out her eyes with a pair of dull metal scissors. She cannot be forced to witness such ugliness from a man to whom her daughter and she had devoted their entire lives. This is one option—and it does not happen.

In another option, the man offers up his second wife instead. The devil opens his briefcase and there are tens of millions of diamonds inside. The man shakes the devil's hand, and off he goes with the man's second wife! The man trades a few diamonds for a never-ending cup of spirits and he trades a few more diamonds for a whole block of buildings in the city, a place he despises with all its stupid rules and top-buttoned regulations, so he opens a whole strip of brothels and opium dens and other sordid places, and he invades the city with sin. His daughter quickly becomes an addict and a whore, but when her father's second wife left for hell with the devil, she gave her daughter—not by blood, but it isn't about blood, not anymore—all of the wickedness that once belonged in her own heart, and the threads of her evil heart's thorny vines slink around her daughter's veins and she is protected. One day, she will murder her father and usurp his throne. She will free her stepmother from the devil and together they will reign. The city will once again be safe, and they will forever be cited in history books as the saviors not only of the city but of the entirety of Germany. This is another option—and it also does not happen.

In another version, the man gives the devil his one and only daughter, and when the devil leaves and the man opens up the briefcase, it is filled with uranium. The man is only a fool so he doesn't know what uranium is, he doesn't know what power he wields. It looks like any other shiny useless rock so he throws it away. The trash man tosses it in a landfill, and because the devil has given the man all of the earth's uranium, the man has unknowingly saved the world from catastrophe and he is never acknowledged as the hero of prevention because there is no such thing as a hero of prevention. Prevention deserves no accolades. The man mourns his stupidity for trading such an apt girl for a pile of goddamn rocks. Even worse, the evil in the second wife's heart returns without the protective aura of the little girl's goodness, and one day, long in the future, she will torture the man worse than Guantanamo and leave him there to rot. This is another option—and obviously, it does not happen, either.

In another version, the second wife offers herself to the devil instead. The devil is insulted and leaves with his briefcase. The man resumes his begging and he beats his second wife and his daughter and it is a Shakespearean tragedy in that house. This is a more likely option—and the devil considers it carefully. Ultimately, he declines.

In another version, the man says, "But she will not be young forever. Come back when she reaches her sixteenth year." The man looks to the briefcase. "Let's say you give me one quarter of what's in that briefcase and if I can triple the value of what you give me, I can keep my daughter and give you all the profits. If I can't do it, she's yours."

The devil thinks over this negotiation and says, "You're being ridiculous. What do I have to win in this wager?"

The man says, "My daughter, my failure, and my shame."

"As if that's enough. Plus," the devil says, "I have to wait an entire decade to collect."

The man becomes keen and says, "Take my second wife here as collateral. She is pretty enough and she's a good worker."

The devil says, "No way. Here's the way I see it. I take

you to hell with me until your daughter is 'of age'—whatever that means—and then I'll release you and take her."

The man hardly blushes, pumps out, "Absolutely—" and the devil takes this is an eager yes and they pop into hell and the second wife and the daughter live many years in peace. When she arrives at her sixteenth birthday, the devil arrives right on schedule and says, "I was never going to take you, dear girl. Your purity would only liven my heart," and the daughter says, "A deal is a deal," and her father is returned to earth and the devil becomes soft and dahlias inject the dull city with vibrancy and tourism. This is close to what happens, but not quite.

*

There is a man begging on the otherwise clean streets of the city. He has consumed so many spirits he can barely hold his sign up straight. It is, in fact, upside-down. No one stops to help him, so he takes himself another mouthful of vodka.

TWO KNOCKS

ốc, cốc.

Ai đó?

Mật.

Mật nào?

Mật khẩu của bạn đã bị đổi!

GET WELL SOON, XOXO

*O**nce,* the devil becomes quite sick. His face pales to a softer hue, a quieter one, but who can the devil call in for a sick day? It's not like he's got a roster of back-ups or something. This poor devil has no one. This poor devil is lonely. And he is sick. Nothing is worse than being sick and lonely and a devil, too. The devil wears a fitted suit and rallies enough spirit to pick up his clipboard and start at it.

First the devil visits a farmer and his wife, who is heavy with child.

"Please," the farmer says. "Take me instead."

The devil hasn't even revealed his identity yet, which is what he likes most—the big reveal: sequins and fireballs, party favors and what not. "You're messing this all up," the devil says. He pouts. "There's an order to things, you see, and you can't just go messing up the process."

Everyone stands still, waiting for the other to move, and they are nearly at that breaking point, where gravity is just about to pull everything apart, and the devil says, "Let's just start over, shall we?" He goes out the front door and slams it shut.

Meanwhile, the wife runs over and locks the bolt.

Meanwhile, the devil knows he has been outwitted.

Meanwhile, the farmer laughs and the devil sneezes and the wife hands him a potful of butter and a cup's worth of whiskey. Wait: when did the devil land back in the house? Why, with his sneeze, of course! The wife lets out a cry and surely it is time for a baby to be born. This is no place for a devil, especially a germy one, and so the devil downs this witch's potion and finds himself better, much better.

But an offer is an offer and you should never offer the devil something for anything at all, so the devil takes the farmer with him, and they all lived the rest of their lives with simple happiness and joy.

TWO KNOCKS

*nock, knock.*

Who's there?

A broken pencil.

A broken pencil who?

Never mind, it's pointless.

THE WITCH AT BLACKBIRD POND

1.

*O*nce, there was an old crone. Heartache and years have turned her into this old crone with dry skin and gunpowder hair.

All around her, people called her a witch: she didn't understand how it happened.

They threw rocks at her cats and knocked sneers at her face.

But what they didn't know was how beautiful she was when she was still young. She may have even been an enchanted princess, who knows!

They did not know that this will become their fate, too, one day far, far away.

The future is too far away for anyone to see.

They lived around a pond known for crows and its other inky birds.

2.

Or, it was a real witch who made her this way, an old crone with dry skin and gunpowder hair.

Although her eyes were halcyon, the blackness of the

water made them sheen with reflective shadow. Sitting pond-side, she retrospected and sighed at fate and its murky choices.

3.

Or, she has always been this way. She has neither been young nor beautiful. Nor has she ever strived for such paltry goals.

4.

Because happily ever after is only another name for insomnia.

5.

Or, she's there, at the bottom of the pond, and it was her sadness that turned the water so dark and vengeful, a water that will never forgive, never again.

6.

Riddle me this one: What the fuck is wrong with being a witch?

She has thousands of Internet friends; they wish her happy birthday, like they understand the language of her damage.

7.

Or, because she didn't sink, the wind kissed her ashes a million times, each one a tiny farewell.

TWO KNOCKS

 *nock, knock.*

Who's there?

Ima Peeka

Ima Peeka who?

No—Ima Peekachu—through the keyhole.

THE TALE OF THE GIRL
CRAWDADDY

T̶he devil can take on many different forms: never forget that. This is a cautionary tale, so pay attention: the devil has many faces, many bodies, many modulations in voice. Sometimes, she is unrecognizable in her fruitful guises, which she can change lickety-split. Everyone assumes the devil is a man, but this isn't some Biblical magic story about angels falling from the sky, from the grace of goodness. No, this one is entirely true. And of all people, I should know—it happened to me, once.

*

Once, I was sitting in my house, and where was this? Why, in a land where snow extends like the desert is full of sand. My house at this time was modest in size and structure. By structure, I mean the roof had ten thousand leaks and I had ten thousand bowls to catch the slow leak of snow rushing into water, but only when I put more wood into the fire, which was hot, which melted the snow, which filled the bowls, and I could be warm and flooded or cold and still flooded. This was my life, wet and without hope.

But what did I care, really? I was just a girl craw daddy in a silver glass dress—only, the water was not salted and

I couldn't breathe without salinity to salve my pumps and my brain was only so big back then that sometimes, I didn't even mind.

Everyone called me Girl Craw Daddy, lest people think I'm a boy. Not all craw daddies are boys, you know. That's just plain illogical.

Like I was saying, I was sitting in my house, not bothering anyone but myself with my quiet suffering, and then—there was a knock at the door. No one has ever come visit me before. I could hardly even understand that a knock meant someone was at the door, that someone was on the other side. But the knocking became aggressive and I became scared—such a strange sound, as though murder by sledgehammer might be happening and right outside— oh yes, I was certainly frightened, not for myself, per se, but for what might be occurring so closely to me that I might be to blame, and so I opened the door, and this, perhaps, was my first mistake. The first of twenty-thousand more and a prawn can only buy so many bowls: at some point, even the bowl makers cut you off.

"Girl Craw Daddy," the bowl maker had said to me, "I can only make so many bowls in a day, and every day you ask for more and every day you cannot pay for all the bowls I make. You are not worth my time."

And when I went to the next bowl maker, he would repeat the same thing, like bowl makers have ready-made scripts for small prawns like me, who can drag only a limited number of kronas at a time, there being no pockets on my dress and I was not wise enough to buy a coat. I dragged my small body from one bowl maker to another, until I had ten thousand bowls, but not a one would give me more, all citing the same logic, using the same words, nothing but rejections through and through.

So I opened the door with a big claw hand, and in rushed a frail little lady dressed in a fairy black dress. Her hair was a jumble of peppercorns and her tongue was a paring knife, that's how sharp it was—or, is, still, because she doesn't die, apparently, even after being killed who knows how many times, but surely more times than there were bowls in my house and that was how I knew there was something sinister in this little old lady. And yes, there was something sinister indeed.

*

Because my parents abandoned me the moment I was born, I have issues, sure. Wouldn't you, too?

*

"Look how you've grown," said the old lady, and her hand transformed into a red claw and she smoothed it against my silver glass dress.

Nor was I some fool, save for the hope that this old magic lady might be some form of family, lost for too long: but me or her? Who has been lost? Who waits to be found. "Who are you?" I asked, not without suspicion.

"Oh," the old lady gasped. She put her two claws to her face to display her awe, and then she clasped me tightly and I felt warm perhaps for the first time. "Girl Craw Daddy," she said, "I have a proposition for you."

*

The contract, she'd insisted, was as transparent as my dress is glass.

"A series of simple trades," the old lady said. "This for that and a little bit of that for this." She snapped her claws together. "Details, details. Those we can smooth out later."

Later—later.

*

The old lady wove through the bowls: and for a solid roof, she gave me a human body; and for a human body, she gave me thirty-five years; and for thirty-five years, she gave me love; and for love, I sacrificed nothing. "In thirty-five years," the old woman said, "we will meet again.

She stopped quite suddenly, in front of a mirror by my door, said, "Look here." She nodded her wrinkled face towards the mirror, took a claw to the glass, said, "Aren't I just so fair?" And I, too, glanced into the mirror. There, I saw a woman who could have been my mother, and next to her, a human woman with a girlish body, all awkward and lovely. "Now we must derive a better name than Girl Craw Daddy, mustn't we? You're not even a craw daddy anymore."

I looked more carefully at myself in the mirror. It was impossible to believe we could be the same, my girlish human reflection and me. My silver glass dress shone like a fairy tale, and I could imagine a happy life. "Thank you," I said, and the old woman said, "Don't go thanking me just yet," and quick as a button, she was gone.

*

With human hands, I gathered the bowls and emptied the melted snow from each one. I dried each one and made columns and columns of bowls. Of the ten thousand, I set two aside, one for myself and one for the love I was certain to meet. As for the rest, I returned them to their bowl-makers, and since I hadn't paid for them anyway, there wasn't any huge to-do, just dirty old men eager to help such a beautiful young lady. Even my dress was unrecognizable to them. Even the bowls they once made seemed different, foreign, like they were not the men who had once forged them, they were light in my hands, almost floating, and when I released them, they did not fall to the ground but swirled around me until all that remained of them was glittery pearls, and those fell from the air and affixed themselves to my glass dress until it was no longer a glass dress but a dress composed entirely of pearls.

The bowl makers, who were usually so stingy, marveled, and soon the news of my miracle traveled through the city, and soon the Prince whose name was Charming wanted to meet me. Me! Just a girl craw daddy called Girl Craw Daddy: I was to have a private audience with Charming!

*

Yes, yes, you know how the story goes: first comes love and then comes marriage and I never pushed any baby carriages, but only because one of our many nannies and servants volunteered every day to take the children out to play. Charming was just as charming as his name promised and ours was a happy life, which we knew would be forever and ever—but one frosty night, there was a soft knock at the door.

Oh, I knew who it was. The years had not aged her in the least: she was as old and haggardly as she was the day we met. "About those details," the old woman said.

The old woman took a quick turnabout and danced a little ditty with jazz hands and popping feet, and when I saw her face again, it was mine: my face, the face I had grown so accustomed to in the mirror, my humanity: thirty-five years of it to the dot.

"Have you noticed," we said as one, "that you have not wrinkled in thirty-five years?"

We nodded.

"And Charming?" we asked.

"Him?" we asked, pointing to the mirror, and so I saw my husband's face.

"Charming!" we yelled out—for my beloved had been dead for nearly a decade now—but in the mirror he was as handsome as ever, and youthful, and full of spirit.

"Girl Craw Daddy," he said, reached his hand through the mirror, and caressed not our face but hers. I watched as she stepped into the mirror.

"Now look," she said, and so I looked, and it was no longer my young and beautiful face, and yet nor was it again a girl craw daddy face.

*

When I walk, it is with a cane. I don't need it, it's all a hoax. When I knock at your door, open it. Offer me some tea and biscuits and I will make you an excellent deal. I will give you love and cloak beauty atop your heinous body. I will give you what was once mine—glorious, glorious mine—and in time, I will collect. We will collect. My Charming waits for me to save him from that sneaky devil, now do we have a deal?

TWO KNOCKS

ốc, cốc.

Ai đó?

Mít.

Mít nào?

Mít đừng hỏi nữa, mở cửa cho tôi vào đi!

THE SCORE

*O*nce, there is a poor farmer man and his wife and they have three daughters. Every day, the farmer man would go out to sow and plow and harvest, while his wife cared for the home. As for the daughters, why, they would go to the market and sell their father's crops—all except for the youngest daughter, who stayed at home to spin wool into yarn, which she would dye into the purest colors any eye could see. These are the most popular items the older sisters sell from their small canopy stall.

Daily the youngest daughter tends her sheep, and she sings them sweet songs and pets them gently. She thanks them for their coats before she commences the sheering. Now it is not that her family does not love her, but they laugh at her nonetheless. "Silly girl," the wife says and shakes her head roughly, "what man will ever marry a girl who talks to sheep?"

The two eldest daughters giggle and sneer their pretty faces.

"Lucky we have you two," the farmer man says.

Every penny the family has ever profited is kept in an ivory chest. All in all, there are two thousand twenty-five gold coins inside. The farmer man intends this to be the dowry for his girls: the two eldest would receive one thousand each, and the youngest, well, she was a hopeless case, so there was no need for them to save for her. Indeed once the chest held a tidy three thousand gold coins, but sometimes wives need new dresses and powders and men need to keep their wives pleased. Furthermore, it is no secret that the youngest daughter's fibers are the finest in the land, and so it is wisdom that borrows from her dowry, not selfishness, for though the farmer man worked very hard, his crops alone could hardly feed his family, much less clothe and cover all the rest of their basic human needs—and some excesses, too.

*

Now comes the day when the daughters are of age to be wed, all three of them, but of course, the youngest shouldn't—as her parents would say—expect much, given the state of her dowry. "You'd be a hopeless case anyway," the mother says. "Even if you had a full five thousand gold coins, no man could carry on with a silly girl like you."

The old farmer man adds, "You point me to one single man out there who would have you, and I'll—well—I'd give up farming and take up weaving!"

Everybody laughs, even the youngest daughter, at the preposterous image of the old farmer man steering a loom. When the laughter fades to false smiles, the three daughters leave.

*

After walking an entire league, the eldest sister says, "Pooey! We have already walked an entire league, and where are all the fine princes?"

The middle sister says, "I'd be satisfied with just a

knight. No need to aim so high, sister."

The youngest sister is quiet.

And so she passes a nest of bees, and honey falls from their hive like dew: slowly, with intention. The youngest sister dips her finger into the sugary nectar and tastes it. Her lips develop a gentle smile.

"Look there," the middle sister says, and she points to the beehive about ten steps away.

"We should bash it with sticks until all the bees die and then we shall eat all the honey and color our lips with their limp stingers," the eldest sister says.

"Yes, yes!" the middle sister says, and she starts running.

"No," the youngest sister says. She catches the middle sister's dress and pulls. Like a rubber band, the middle sister falls back. "These bees have done nothing to you. They're just living their little lives, nothing special. Whereas you two, well, you two have love and adventure and babies in your futures, why would you bother with such little bees?"

And so the three sisters walk around the beehive, and they are just so grateful.

Who? Who is so grateful?

Such grace, too.

She says, "Little bees, keep on, keep on! My sisters have already run far away, and so you will all remain in safety. Fly and buzz and stir out some honey." And the bees swirl around the youngest sister, their little furry hairs give her own russet hair buoyancy and curls, and her skin accepts their yellow dye to suit. She is a marvel.

✳

They walk another league and arrive at a lake that is at least seven leagues in circumference, which is quite far indeed, much less for three sisters, two of whom are dressed for a marriage proposal and one who is dressed sensibly. In the lake swim golden ducks, ducks whose feathers are so auric they look as though they should drown under such glinting weight.

The eldest sister says, "Look at those stupid ducks."

The middle sister makes a sinister face. "I want to throw all these stones at them."

The youngest sister is silent.

The middle sister bends at her slight waist to collect flat grey stones.

The elder sister says, "No, there," and points to a boulder. "We shall sink them all with one good bowling push!"

And two sisters move towards the boulder, but the youngest sister says, "No, sisters, you shan't do such a thing! Why, look at those little yellow ducks. Pray, tell, what have they done to you? You will have such joy and pleasure in your future lives with your handsome princes. What due happiness will these ducks have in comparison?"

Hence the three sisters trudge their way through marsh and swamp, and buckets of mud cling to their shoes and lace hosiery. Their skin, so moistened with such ardent travail, twinkles.

Shining, they are beautiful.

Feathers or flesh: what division!

*

Alas, far in the distance, the sisters spy a marble castle, its envious green.

The two elder sisters begin to run.

The youngest sister only walks.

And so she passes an anthill, and she says, "Little ants,

little ants, keep on scurrying. My sisters have already run far away, and so you will all remain in safety."

The ants, recognizing in the youngest sister an altruism they have never felt before, crawl up and around her body and when she finally looks down, they have linked their small legs into a magenta gown which gloves her lithe form into magnificence.

*

When the youngest sister reaches the castle, the two elder sisters are trying to haul a marble stallion, using all their might to pull the immobile beast: an untamable thing, so suspended. "Help us," the eldest sister says, "you stupid sister." Now it is not of normal fashion for either sister—of the three—to speak so cruelly, for theirs is a loving family, but these are sisters who have been on an odyssey for weeks, and they are hungry and they are tired, and venom is most potent: it kills like a poison comb, and the youngest sister's hair is a bird's nest.

But wait: what of her lovely gown and glowing skin? Oh, they don't have the temperance to notice such paltry things on a sister so doomed for spinsterhood. They can think only of themselves and the wealth this marble stallion will bring them and their dowries, if only they could move the damn thing. It is terribly heavy.

"Youngest sister," the elder says, "help us and we will share the profits for your dowry." The elder, it appears, has a brain, but it is not too wise.

"Eldest sister," the youngest sister says and pauses for just two seconds too long.

"Hurry it up now," the middle sister demands. "The sun is nearly setting and we have a long distance to travel."

"Use your brain, dummy," the eldest declares, although

it is unclear which sister she is addressing. "We will sell this heavy beast at the nearest village."

"But," the youngest interjects, "we have not passed a single village and we have travelled quite far already. Perhaps there are no villages so many leagues from our dear home. Perhaps there is only this very castle, and perhaps the owners of this castle will not appreciate our thievery."

"Your brain, stupid," the eldest says, and this time it is clear she means the youngest sister.

"Yes," the youngest says, "my brain suggests we knock on the palace door. As you have said, the sun is nearly setting and we must rest, especially if we—" and by *we* she means only the two elder sisters, for she wants to bear no guilt for such a sin as theft "—are to push this statue all the way to the nearest town, and who knows how far that may be!"

The eldest sister walks up to the youngest sister and smacks her in the head. "Good thinking."

The two elder sisters walk up to the palace door. The youngest remains by the marble stallion. She reaches up to the stallion's face and pets it kindly. "Dear beast," she says, "what I would give for you to escape the torture my sisters promise you." She looks at it with care and suddenly, the marble begins to crack and the stallion draws itself back into life: green and mighty, and it gallops toward the forest.

The two elder sisters run up to the youngest and hit her repeatedly for her folly. They do not notice the magic her hands have just transferred. They do not even think of it. "Doomed!" they yell as one. "We are doomed."

✳

While the elder sisters remain forlorn, the youngest makes her way to the palace door and knocks. It glides open and a servant comes forth. The youngest sister curtsies her head low and the elder sisters have bloated noses from crying. They are a sore sight for eyes, even for a servant. "Come," he says, and the trio follows him into the palace. It is more extravagant inside than the outside might suggest, and the outside is composed of pure jade, so one can only imagine what the interior portends. Lavishness coats everything with sparkle and glow.

For once, the elder sisters are quiet. They are stunned.

But to the youngest sister, it is only a house. A house with much more bombast than her own, to be sure, and so she says, "We three are merely peasant sisters, but we beg an audience with the owner of this grand estate such that we may beg, yet again, for a warm bed to rest and perhaps a piece of bread to fill our hunger."

"Fool," the middle sister says.

"Imbecile," the eldest sister agrees, and she slaps the youngest sister without shame. "Forgive this girl. She knows nothing. She is just a stupid peasant girl who we allowed to travel with us, but it is true that we are quite tired and need a place to repose."

The servant bows his head towards their apparent graces, says, "Indeed."

*

The sisters are served a fine dinner of stuffed duck—which the youngest declines—and honey tarts, which the youngest sister eats and eats her dinner's worth. Neither the King nor the Prince joins them for dinner, but only the youngest sister notices their absence. As a servant serves her a tenth honey tart, she says, "Pray, may we three sisters make acquaintance with the masters of this fine palace?" He says nothing but steps back many times until he is gone past the doorway, out of view, and then he takes off running to the King and the Prince. Someone eating honey tarts is someone special, the poor servant doesn't know why, but he has a message to deliver and he must deliver it with the greatest urgency.

❊

Each sister is given a separate chamber. The eldest sister's room is blush; the middle sister's room shimmers; and youngest sister's room contains countless mirrors, reflections pinging to and fro without concern, with whim. When she smiles, the room beams with pleasure.

But in the light of morning, the eldest sister finds her room is just some painted mud and the middle sister's room is polished nickel, but the youngest, her room spins sun rays around her and she floats under all that warmth.

❊

"Welcome," the King says.

All three sisters swoon when the King steps to the side and the handsomest Prince in all of the world comes forth. He bows to each, and he stops at each sister, takes her hand in his, and kisses it gently.

"Well," says the King, "now that we are all acquainted, let us get this party going. My son here is in search of a bride, and all of you seem apt enough, but I will only wed him to she who can perform three small tasks to better my old life. First, remove this mountain from my view." The King points out the window. There is a very big mountain indeed, and the King would like to watch the sun crest over not a mountain but just the horizon itself. "You will each have from sunrise to the following morning's sunrise to fulfill this task. The eldest will go first, for obvious reasons."

What's the obvious reason?

And so the eldest departs. When the sun rises the next morning, a whole cavalcade comes out to greet a big pile of unmoved rocks. The eldest sister throws her body against a boulder; it doesn't seem to care.

"Your turn." The King nods at the middle sister.

When the sun rises the next morning, the whole cavalcade returns and again, the rocks are still there, as much a mountain as ever.

"Your turn." The King nods at the youngest sister. Whereas the youngest sister wants to overanalyze things and say the King was rallying for her all along, this is just fruitless thinking.

*

By sundown, the task is impossible. Even with the King's blessing—which is an unreliable source, to be sure—the youngest sister has managed to lower the mountain by barely a meter or two. See, the youngest sister being wiser than her two elders, began not at the bottom of the mountain but its top, and from there, she pushed rocks down until the mountain began to recede into the flat earth, but only by an imperceptible amount. By the time the sun has fully set and the moon begun its ascent, she is without hope. She falls to the ground and weeps.

Along walks a small ant, small especially against the enormity of all those boulders she had tirelessly tumbled down the mountainside, and she says, "Pretty sister, pretty sister, why do you woe?"

The youngest sister might have not heard the small ant, but she did, and so she said, "I'm to move this entire mountain by sunrise if I am to marry the Prince, but as you can see, my sister ant, this task is not for one sister to do alone, for it is impossible."

The small ant crawls up the youngest sister's arm and into the small of her ear. There, she whispers, "Rest, dear sister. Sleep and when the sun rises, all will be as you desire." And so the youngest sister falls asleep and when the sun stirs the trumpets sing and here comes the King riding on a great stallion and the entire cavalcade pursues.

✳

It's true that an ant can lift up to one thousand times her small body weight, and if it were but one ant, such a feat might seem insignificant, but vast is a sister ant's army—notably vast.

So deep was the youngest sister's slumber from the tire of the day that she did not feel the very earth beneath her move.

✳

"Next," says the King, "at the bottom of this swamp sits three pearls. They belonged to my late wife." The King removes his crown, as does the Prince, in a moment of quiet mourning. "I would like them back." The King eyes the two elder sisters. "You're behind on the count."

The King looks out upon his unobstructed view, impressed by all that he owns.

✳

The eldest sister has weak lungs and she forgot her inhaler. She fails.

The middle sister dives and she dives. She touches a pearl and it is very large. She cannot pick it up with her limited breath, but she tries and no one can fault her for not trying. Finally, she unlodges it and gathers the beastly thing in her arms and struggles against gravity to rise to the surface with it. Turns out it was just a tortoise shell that had been rubbed clean in all that swampy gunk. The middle sister collapses on the thing: such is her exhaustion.

The youngest sister is surely stricken with fear and grief, but alas, she lifts the skirt of her dress and steps into the swamp. Immediately, she turns into a golden duck and so she dives into the water and her eyes are clear: she can see through all the mud and fish and she finds the first pearl easily. She uses her flaxen beak to hold it and she paddles her way to the surface. Once she reaches the shore, she transforms once again into the youngest sister. She drops a pearl at the King's feet and goes back into the water. Twice more she repeats her ritual of metamorphosis, and twice more she is victorious.

*

That night there is a ball, and although all three sisters look elegant and fine, the Prince chooses to dance only with the youngest, which is the one he preferred all along anyway.

The King laughs, "Ho! Ho! Ho!" because he is happy.

*

Finally, it is morning, and the King says, "For too long, there has only been silence here, and you three sisters have granted me joy. Let the palace sing with song." He pats his robust belly. "And I want you to sing it. The best shall take the Prince's hand."

"No, no," the Prince says. "You said she who completed all three tasks, and Father, only one has completed two of the three." The Prince says, "To me, only one shall compete."

And the King goes, "Don't be a fool, son. The first two tasks I wanted just for me. This final task will bring the entire kingdom joy. The final task is the only important one to me." And the King goes, "See girls? It's an open race, now let's see what you three can do."

So the youngest sister is handicapped now. For her entire life, she has known only yarn and thread. While her eldest sisters took music lessons—to become well-rounded future wives to important men—the youngest sister talked to her little sheep. Fool!

✳

The King throws another ball, and the Prince must dance with all three sisters this time. To his great surprise, the two eldest hold their toes pointed and light, whereas the youngest—having never been trained the art of dance— fumbles. How strange that he should not have noticed this just one night before.

When it is time, the eldest takes the stage, and there, she sings a magnificent aria. The crowd weeps.

Next, the middle sister sits at the harpsichord and plays a playful fugue and the people dance and then they rejoice.

Finally, the youngest sister steps forward. She can neither sing nor play any instruments, save a loom, a spindle, and some knitting needles, and so she holds one nickel needle up and in fly a swarm of bees and she moves her needle and they buzz an entire symphony and the entire palace blazens with life. The statues melt into animals, and they stampede into the ballroom to join the party. And it is a party indeed.

✳

So, surely, the Prince marries the youngest sister, and the King takes on the two eldest sisters as chambermaids, because he is not a brutal King: he is a kind one. The eldest is given a room made of swamp mud, and the middle is given a room made of stone. When he is bored, and Kings are so often bored, he has his way with them, and they do not complain because he is the King. No one ever complains around a King.

TWO KNOCKS

*K*nock, knock.

Who's there?

Budweiser.

Budweiser who?

But-why's-her jokes gotta bee so bad?

A HORSE'S CROWN

*O*nce, there is a princess, her handmaid, and a talking horse. The handmaid rides a horse as well, but it is old and ugly. They are on the way to a great prince's castle; this road is long and arduous. This is the wedding procession.

Suddenly, the handmaid says, "Stop," and they all stop. They don't freeze in place or anything—this isn't a children's game—but they halt all the same. The handmaid says, "Get off your stupid talking horse. I want to ride it now."

"Well what shall I ride then?" the princess asks. "All my life I have only ridden one horse. Barney is my only companion in life, I cannot let you ride him."

The handmaid gets off her horse and pushes the princess into a mud puddle. When she rises, it is not graceful. When she mounts the old and ugly horse, she is not lithe. No, she is soaked with goop and slides all over the place.

❋

So a princess, her handmaid, and a talking horse walk into a bar.

"Three beers, please."

They order another round, and then they go to sleep.

Later, when they reach the castle, they knock at the palace door. No one answers. The castle is entirely sedate, not a ghoul in sight.

*

The prince does not greet them immediately because he is out hunting pretty pale doves—those pests!—in the great forests surrounding his castle. After many hours, he returns and the handmaid gets off the fancy horse and curtsies all the way down to the prince's knees. But the handmaid is not a lady. She looks like a jester, except that the rouge on her cheeks is more subdued. When she lowers her head in a bow, the prince can see chiggers cling onto her matted hair, lest they fall into gravity.

Yet—this is the way of arranged marriages.

And so they married, the handmaid and the prince.

The king is unhappy.

His queen is dead, but still, she mourns and flowers pipe out from her grave. Her tears fertilize them.

The prince is unhappy. All day long he pouts.

The real princess is banished to servitude.

Even the talking horse is appalled.

Someone is satisfied, though: can you guess who?

*

There was once a princess who would adorn Barney's neck with a string of thick pearls and braid ruby flowers in his mane.

*

After the ceremony, the crown princess tells the prince to cut off Barney's head and mount it on the wall of the kitchen, such that her handmaid may have a companion when she sleeps by the oven for warmth.

✣

In the name of altruism.

✣

For purposes of clarity, the old princess is now the hand-maid; the handmaid is now the princess. Their identities have not changed. Their personalities have not swapped. This is an exchange in title alone.

✣

Except title *is* identity. Or, it can be. There is a relationship there, and it is not tenuous.

✣

Time moves, but patiently.

One day, the handmaid mourns to her horse head, says, "Oh Barney!"

And Barney says, "Your mother would be so disappointed. Her heart will unravel its chambers."

The blood has dried around the horse's neck. Nails adhere his skin to lacquered wood. When she pets Barney's desiccating mane, her hand is a milky stream of elegance. Barney leans his horse face into her smell, and a nail pops out of its hole. Barney bleeds and he bleeds and they both think this is the end. Everything is hopeless.

But—because they live inside magic, the handmaid picks up the nail, shoves it into an unbloody patch of skin, and the horse is healed and there isn't even a mess to clean up!

✣

The princess is cruel to her handmaid because when their titles were reversed—well, reciprocation is merely an ethical suggestion, not a requirement.

*

Oh, nothing special, just some whipping and some caning. Just audio torture and a cement floor. The handmaid does not even have a blanket to call her own.

*

Before, blankets crammed tight with goose.
　　Now, she must braid her own hair.
　　The water for her bath is not boiled first.

*

Starvation, too.

*

One day the king notes the goodness of the thin pretty maid-girl. He commands her as his own, not like a concubine or mistress or anything, and he is a good king, a kind one. He gives her proper chambers and a simple smock with pockets.

*

Meanwhile, the prince will not fuck his new bride. She arrived with bugs leeched everywhere. He will not let her into his bed, but her chambers are lush so what does she care?

When the princess strikes the handmaid with an iron bar, the bruises form and then heal immediately, and so she must strike harder the next time, and the next, and the handmaid does not cry out for help. The horse watches it all, helpless.

✻

When will the hero arrive and save the disguised princess? Already she is surrounded by royalty; figure it out already, please!

✻

The handmaid cries to her horse, and pearls fall from her eye sockets. It is torture, and there is blood everywhere. The handmaid drops the pearls into a basin and washes them. She forces a needle and thread through. She is making Barney a new crown, but that requires many, many more tears.

✻

When the handmaid cries, Barney closes his eyes and pushes his head to the side. He cannot witness such woe.

He laments, "Your mother would be so disappointed. Her heart will unravel its chambers."

But this only causes the handmaid to weep, and the pearls become so large that they rip the tender skin beneath her eyes.

✻

Hard to follow the logic, but when Barney makes her cry, her wounds do not heal. It is only when the princess torments her that the fabric of magic falls over the handmaid's body with elixir.

✻

Ahoy! Who comes this way? A royal procession?

Light the chandeliers and behead us some goose! Tonight, there will be a feast of welcoming!

✳

The sight of her old flag from her chamber window sends the princess into a frenzy.

Insects line the floor, her miniature army.

But they will not follow her commands.

✳

Of course, the handmaid does not know about her mother's arrival. She is in the kitchen, preparing for a feast. She walks by the talking horse and pets his mane. He nuzzles her face and his skin does not tear. Trumpets declare the arrival of royalty and the handmaid runs to her chambers to change her smock. Even servants must look presentable when a feast is at hand.

The handmaid disrobes and re-robes, and her beauty emits enough glow to illuminate the darkest dungeon.

She grabs a box and runs back into the kitchen, says to the horse, "This is for you." She opens the box and a crown of pearls descends upon his head.

And still, Barney says, "Your mother would be so disappointed. Her heart will unravel its chambers."

And then, "Thank you, my princess. When your agony is washed away, only the precious remains."

✳

The queen is anxious to see her daughter, who she is told is terribly ill at the moment.

The king and prince receive her. She asks if her daughter is yet with child. The prince will not look at her. He seems bored, but really, he is frightened of the revelation that he has not copulated, that he will give his father and mother-in-law no child. *How odd,* the prince thinks, *that a daughter can look so different from her mother.*

How unfair, the king himself thinks, *that a woman so fair birthed such an ugly girl.*

The king whistles for his handmaid. She carries in a carafe of wine and curtsies, first before the king, then the prince, then her mother.

And so it is, the queen's heart unravels in its chambers and the handmaid's true identity is revealed.

*

Don't call it revenge.

Call it justice.

A handmaid's head mounted next to the talking horse.

Barney never liked her anyway. He spits right in her face, and mites crawl out of her eyes. They pinch onto her flesh, lest they, too, are crushed under the weight of air.

TWO KNOCKS

*nock, knock.*

Who's there?

Not your wife.

LIKE SUGAR ON THE TONGUE

*S**he** may be an old crone of a witch, but when others see her, they only see a homely baker girl. She is a confectioness, and no one makes such luscious treats in all of Praha. They absolutely dissolve right against the moisture of the tongue and all the proper buds are activated to taste perfection. It can only be called perfection.

But during the night, when she does her baking and the rest of Praha sleeps in their flats or their palaces, she shakes off the skin of the homely baker and sprinkles its remnants into the dough. This is her secret and ever-lasting ingredient. This is what makes the people delight. All night long, the crone works in her old crone body: she mixes the dough and she portions each piece just right and she bakes and she times it and she inspects them and when it is time—and her timing is clockwork—she cools them on a rack. She makes icings. She makes glazes. She makes hardened shells for the ones who deserve it.

*

Before the first crow calls, she is in bed sleeping. Before the sun crests the horizon, she wakes—refreshed and young again—as she does every single day, ever-lasting.

She wakes before all of Praha and she wakes fully clothed in her modest baker clothes, apron and all! She brushes her hair and cleans her teeth and goes downstairs to open shop. It is not a fancy shop, but it sits cleverly at the mouth of the Charles Bridge and so the shop is always full of tourists and locals alike, such is the confected curation that is her modest business.

On any given day, she makes more krona than she could spend if she were to buy ten of the most exquisite dresses for herself, which, of course, she wouldn't. *Of course* she wouldn't. But it wouldn't do any good anyway. She is only a maiden during the day and in the dark of night until the very last moment when she must add her secret ingredient, and then she must become, once again, an old crone witch. Why! If the good Czech people were to know she was really an old crone witch, and the tourists too, no one would support her business—even if she *does* offer the best confections—especially because of it, perhaps.

❊

For an old crone witch, she really is nice. Very nice or too.

❊

One night, the baker is working. It is not yet late, but it is still nighttime. Stars fell in quiet streams. She cracks an egg and lets her fingers act as sieve to collect the yolk, preserve it whole and untethered. She challenges its firmness by rotating her entire hand and just feeling the yolk. And then—there is a knock at the door. At this hour! She walks to the door with yolk still in hand and opens the door.

❊

Once upon a time she was not an old crone witch, she was just a little girl. She had a brother and an old crone witch cooked him in an oven and so the little girl pushed the old crone witch into the oven, too, and she tried to pull her brother free but the old crone witch's weight anchored him down. If she were to burn, the old crone witch reasoned, so too shall he. After some time, it became clear that they must resign, and the little girl closed the oven door, but that did not prevent the torment from being heard, thick as a storm cloud. All that crying made the little girl's hair turn grey and her skin contract into a million wrinkles and magic fluted out of her fingertips, but they were spindles now. She refused to look in a mirror, and it has been many, many years.

*

Because it is not yet too late, she is still a homely baker, nothing exceptional. The door is now fully opened and the person on the other side revealed, and she says, "Oh," because there is no one there. There is no person on the other side of the door.

She returns to her baking.

Soon, she hears more knocking, this time at the window. She opens the window and hoists her torso out of it, but alas, there is no one there.

A quiet layer of snow had fallen and there was not a single track to disrupt its clairvoyance.

She returns to her baking. It is getting on in hours, and soon she must become an old crone witch again, this is what she knows. But the knocking does not return and the baking gets done and she gets into bed and rises and she is a homely baker once again.

＊

She was not destined to be an old crone witch. Nor was she supposed to be a homely baker. When she was a little girl, she was pretty, notably so, but then the tragedy of her brother and her sudden transformation into an old crone witch: even her mother would not have recognized her. She went to sleep, tearful and constantly so, until she was sleeping soundly, and when she woke up, she had transformed yet again: this time into a homely maiden, but inside, she was still just another pretty little girl.

No longer a pretty little girl at all but a grown and homely maiden, she opens up the oven door. Her movement is a secretion of fear: what remains inside. Do bones burn, too?

She opens the oven door and there are three trays of cupcakes baking inside. The other stuff she will learn over time, the other stuff requires magic.

TWO KNOCKS

Knock, knock.

Who's there?

A wooden shoe.

A wooden shoe who?

Eh wooden you like to know!

TWO KNOCKS

nock, knock.

Who's there?

Cash.

Cash who?

No thanks, but do you have any pistachios?

TWO KNOCKS

*K*nock, knock.

Who's there?

Notch.

Notch Who?

Yes, ME!

SILENT NIGHT WITH TEN BILLION FALLING SNOWFLAKES

*O*utside, there is a blizzard huffing around. Snow rumbles like nightmares, and there is not a person in sight. Everyone is reclining beside their warm hearths, telling fairy stories about princesses and frogs and all sorts of funny animals.

Tonight, not a single soul knocks on any door—save the ghouls and monsters—and little girls and little boys should know better than to open their doors to such malicious creatures, even if it is impolite behavior, especially on a night like tonight. On a night like tonight, we might even pity the devil, but we shan't! No, we are wiser than that.

But beware of windows, always beware of those windows.

A JOKE, OF SORTS

*K*nock, knock.

Who's there?

But there is no one. No one is ever there.

ACKNOWLEDGMENTS

The author would like to thank the following journals and anthologies for publishing early versions of the tales in this collection: *Black Candies: Gross and Unlikeable; The Inlander; Threadcount Magazine;* and *Unlikely Stories V.*

✳

The author expresses her forever gratitude to: her alien sister Jackie Wang, Sabrina Gomez, Katie Jean Shinkle, Selah Saterstrom, Kristen Nelson, Kate Bernheimer, Sarah Luna, Lauren Berlant, Richard Greenfield, Tony Stagliano, Justine Wells, Vi Khi Nao, Jess Alexander, Rose Pacault, and—lastly and mostly—Fredrik Farnstrom; their emotional and aesthetic guidance and support made this collection possible. PJ Carlisle deserves the biggest bucket of thanks for his editorial vision and patience. This collection was written with the financial support of New Mexico State University and UC San Diego, and portions were composed at La Ira de Los Dios Artist Residency in Buenos Aires, Argentina, and Buinho Artist Residency in Messejana, Portugal. Finally, the author thanks her students, who provide perpetual inspiration and hope.